D0114413

JoJo's Sweet Adventures

The Terrific Time Twist

JoJo's Sweet Adventures

The Terrific Time Twist

BY JOJO SIWA

Illustrations by Claudia Giuliani

nickelodeon

Amulet Books
New York

Library of Congress Control Number 2021948342
Hardcover ISBN 978-1-4197-5857-7
Paperback ISBN 978-1-4197-5856-0

Book design by The Story Division in consultation with Brenda E. Angelilli
Biographies of historical figures written by Bobby K. Lewis

Printed and bound in U.S.A.
10 9 8 7 6 5 4 3 2 1

Amulet Books are available at special discounts when purchased in quantity for premiums and promotions as well as fundraising or educational use. Special editions can also be created to specification. For details, contact specialsales@abramsbooks.com or the address below.

ABRAMS The Art of Books
195 Broadway, New York, NY 10007
abramsbooks.com

CHAPTER ONE
MYSTERY AT THE MUSEUM

MUSEUM OF HISTORICAL WONDERS
Come on, let's go! This is going to be *ah-MAZING!*
JoJo
Do you think their food court is going to be open?
Miley

Well, if they're not serving food anymore...
Jacob
I *did* bring a metric ton of snacks to make up for it.
Do you ever *not?* We can always rely on you for the chocolatey goodness.
I'm still living off *your* supply from the Sugarpalooza trip.
Oh, wow-- *look!*
Wow.
Did you bring any astronaut ice cream, Jacob?

Oh hey!
I was just giving Saturn a little dust down.
Jada
Of course! We've been wanting to see this *for-e-ver.*
Are you sure it's okay we're here? It seems kind of...not open.
Oh, for sure! My boss said I could do whatever as long as you signed something for him. His daughter's a big fan.
You know I will.

Look at you! You look like Dr. Jada Jekyll with these goggles!
Wait until you see Ms. Jada Hyde. Mwahahaha!
Seriously, how did you get this gig?! **Museum curator** at your age is going to **rock** on your future college applications.
Well, I'm only in charge of one exhibit...but yeah, I can't lie, I love it.
"It actually goes back to the day that I met JoJo at Sugarpalooza.
"My friend Avery's dad owns the place, and we got to take that tour together. Things got...kinda crazy when the place started to...you know, become a **choco-splosion.**

"I've always been interested in science, but when I got the chance to figure out the park's system and fix the delicious problem, Avery's dad told me he'd help me find a gig worthy of a mind like mine."
His words, not mine. I would never brag that much.
If someone *else* says nice things about me, though, hey--what can you do?
You talk about a choco-splosion as if it's a *bad* thing.
Imagine the *perfect* amount of chocolate... and then multiply that by one thousand.
See, I'm a choco-scientist and JoJo is a choco-mathematician. This is why we're friends.
I'm a little bummed that Grace and Kyra couldn't come, though.
I haven't seen them since your concert at the park.

Gah, I knooow. They really wanted to make it.
Grace had to dog-sit for her cousin, so Kyra promised she'd help out. Grace's cousin has **twelve dogs...**
"...which can be quite a handful.

"I dropped BowBow off on our way over here, though, so hopefully she's helping keep those pups in line.
"I figured she could set a good example for the others."
Alllll right, just gotta find...
...the light!
CLICK

Whoa. Wow. Oooooh.
Look at that *absolute beauty.*

I completely agree. Imagine being that thing? I'd never not show off my wings.
I'd be like, "You want to see a wingspan. I am the *queen* of wingspan."
This part actually isn't my exhibit, though.
I'm working on a little something over at the Wing of Time and Space.
We could stop and look at whatever you want on the way, though.
If there's one thing I learned while working here, it's that history is filled with even more beauty than you can ever really comprehend.

This exhibit is about the artwork from Japan's Edo period.
This is one of my favorites to peek at when I'm taking a break from mine.
Ooooh, I've been taking Japanese lessons myself.
I'll be able to watch anime without subtitles in ***no time at all.***
Wow. This is beautiful.
The clothing back then was so gorgeous, too. Imagine us painted in this style?
Well, it could be cool if it was you. But me with the goggles? Hahaha.
I like the goggles.

Hey, so what is the deal with the goggles? Is Saturn really *that* dusty?
Hah, no. I'm just working on some machinery that's a bit...moody. Safety first!
First, check out ***Matsuo Bashō.*** He's like the godfather of haiku.
I heard he could make you a haiku you couldn't refuse.

Anybody hungry yet? All that talk of choco-splosions makes me want to have one in my mouth.
Not gonna introduce your friends, Jada?
Hi, you guys. My name is Caitlin.
I work here, too. You probably walked through my dinosaur exhibit.
Pretty impressive, huh? I've been working on improving the exhibit all summer for my internship.

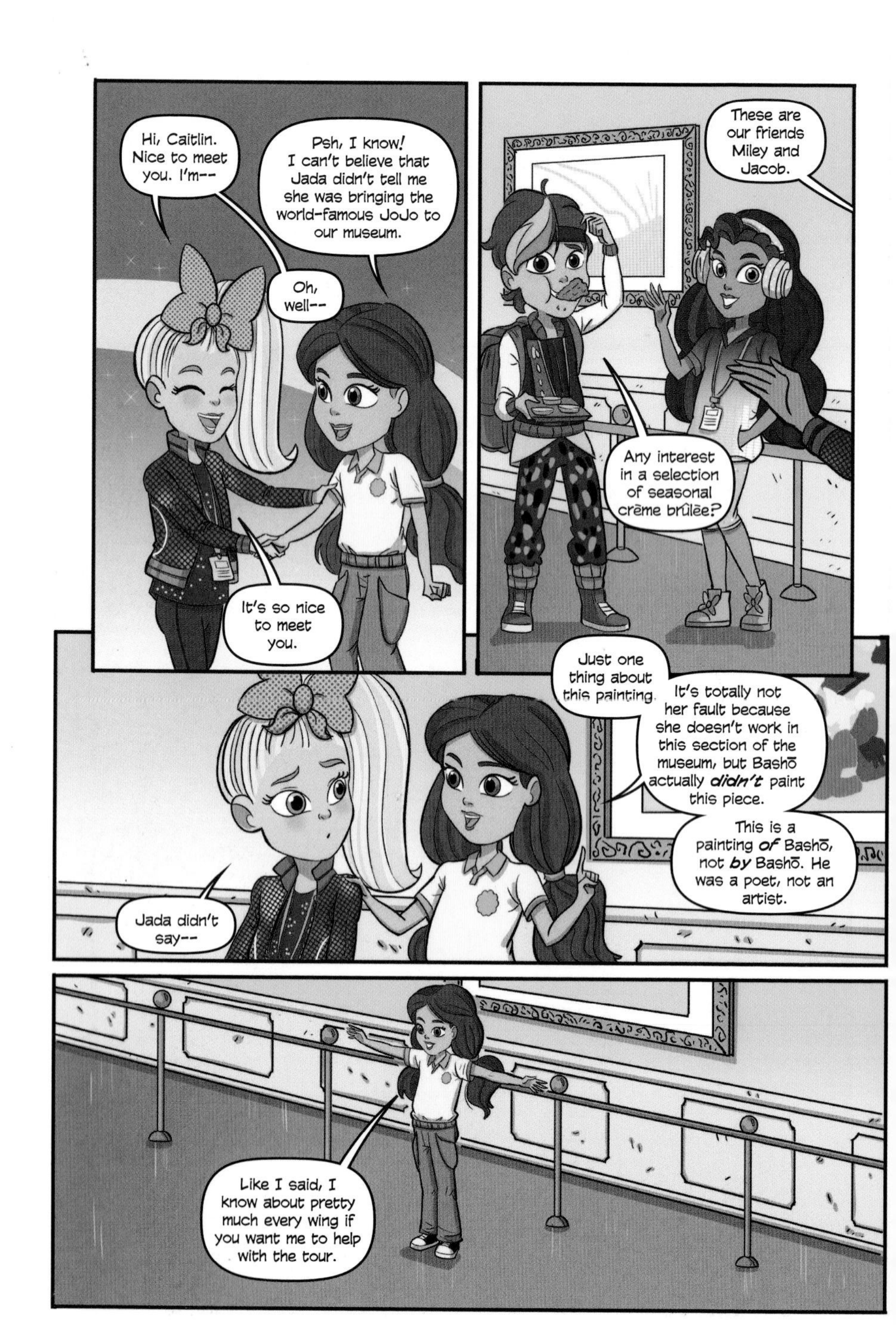
Hi, Caitlin. Nice to meet you. I'm--
Psh, I know! I can't believe that Jada didn't tell me she was bringing the world-famous JoJo to our museum.
Oh, well--
It's so nice to meet you.
These are our friends Miley and Jacob.
Any interest in a selection of seasonal crême brûlée?
Just one thing about this painting.
It's totally not her fault because she doesn't work in this section of the museum, but Bashō actually ***didn't*** paint this piece.
This is a painting ***of*** Bashō, not ***by*** Bashō. He was a poet, not an artist.
Jada didn't say--
Like I said, I know about pretty much every wing if you want me to help with the tour.

Hey, I don't want to be petty, but Bashō for sure was also an artist.
Right over there, some of his haiku have his illustrations on them.
Right, but he didn't paint that painting. It's not a self-portrait.
I didn't say he did, *Caitlin.*
You don't have to be defensive because this isn't your area of expertise, *Jada.*
It makes perfect sense that you'd make a mistake considering what you've been working on.
It's not a big deal.
CRUNCH
CRUNCH

Hey, hey, hey...I think this is just a misunderstanding.
Jada, I think maybe Caitlin misheard you. And Caitlin--
I'm sorry to interrupt, JoJo, but it's actually ***not*** just a misunderstanding.
I don't want to bring up any drama, but Jada and I have something of a ***beef.***
I actually don't have beef with anyone. You've brought the beef.
Actually, ***Jada,*** you've had a problem with me ever since you started working here on your little project.
I know you're insecure about it, which makes you ***very defensive.***
No! I have no beef. I'm only defensive because you keep calling what I'm doing a "little project"!
I don't call YOUR project "little."
Mine is based in reality. Yours is ***fantasy.***
Hey, not to get involved in this riveting drama here... but why do you have a problem with Jada's exhibit?
Go on and tell them. Let's see if ***they*** think you're making a joke out of our museum or not.
How about I just ***show*** them?

Jada...maybe I should just talk to Caitlin.
I don't want to get involved in a fight, but this seems *not* okay.
JoJo, my best friend is Avery... one of the top ten sassiest people on the planet.
I can take Caitlin's drama. And after all is said and done, I bet she'll be singing a different tune.
What do we do here?
Wait, so do we know if the food court is open yet?
What you're about to see is a restored artifact from another time.
It was found on a beach on Long Island fifteen years ago.
No one has been able to determine when it was created...because it couldn't have been created from materials from a single time.
It is thought to be a machine made over a great span of time...or at least from different times.

This, my friends, is...a *time machine.*

Obviously, it doesn't work...but I will say I've made some fixes that have at least gotten some energy moving through it.

Imagine this thing *does* work and all we have to do is figure it out?

Where would *you* want to go if you time-traveled?

I'd want to joust alongside the chivalrous knights from the Middle Ages.
I'd love to do magic tricks with Houdini!
I'd go to the future. I'd like to perform in the first concert after we inhabit Mars.

I don't think this thing can even start up, much less make a trip across the solar system.
This is the kind of fun house attraction that is going to make the museum look *bad.*
How can I put this internship on my college application if they find out that right next to my perfectly-curated dinosaur exhibit was a bogus time machine?!
I mean, like I said, these are just beepers! Someone probably made this out of a broken-down car and old beepers.
You're wrong.
I *told* you this thing starts up. Obviously, it doesn't actually send people into different timelines or it'd be with the *FBI* or something.
But it's an attempt at something incredible and it's worth showing to people.
Is it, though?

Just watch.
WMMM
Jada, be careful...
Of course it didn't *work.* But it's--
Hmm, I haven't seen *that* happen before.
Here, look. Is this *nothing?* I don't think so.
BEEP DEEP BADADA DEEP

SHWAMMM
Are you okay?
Yeah, just a little blinded.
Oh...oh my gosh! JADA!
BLTZ!
JoJo...I don't know what's happening!

HELP ME!
BLTZ!
...Jada?

Jada...
Ohmigosh, what happened?
She just...she vanished.
Oh, come on, you three. You don't really believe this, do you?
It's a *prank.* She knew all it did was light up, so she probably ran off.
I saw her... it looked as if she turned *into* the light.
No way. She's *here.* I know it.
I hope she's right.
Jada, you can come out now! You made your point.
Miley... Jacob... come here.

You have to see this.

CHAPTER TWO
JOJO SIWA, TIME TWISTER

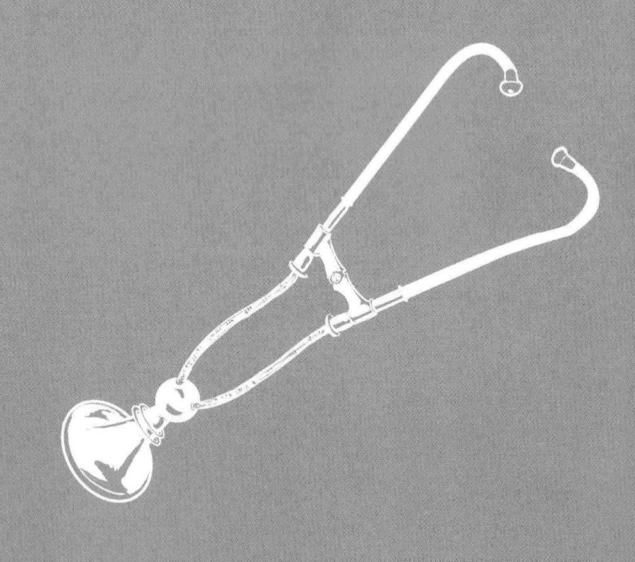

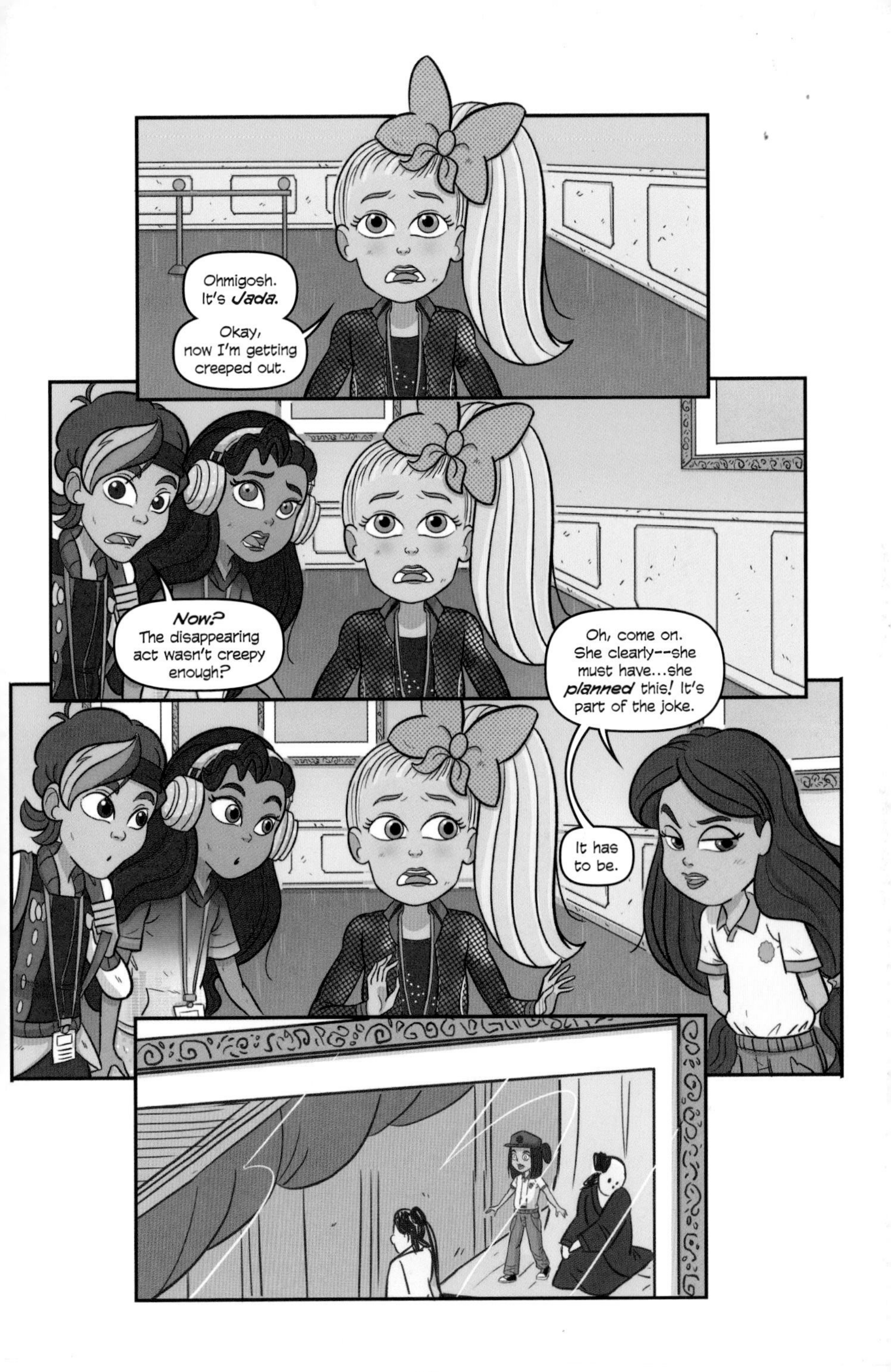
Ohmigosh. It's *Jada.*
Okay, now I'm getting creeped out.
Now? The disappearing act wasn't creepy enough?
Oh, come on. She clearly--she must have...she *planned* this! It's part of the joke.
It has to be.

I'm sorry, but no. Jada would *never* do that.
This is bananas to say *out loud,* but the painting is proof. Jada used the machine to go back in time...
Yeah, right. To what, prove a point?
No. When she realized what was happening, she looked so scared. She was just trying to show that the machine wasn't a piece of junk.
She didn't *mean* to actually leave us...which means that she's in *major* trouble.
"She was tinkering with the buttons and gears and she seemed to have some idea how it worked...in *theory.*"
But I'm worried that she's *stuck* there. If she activated it by mistake, how would she know how to get back?
So *we* have to save her.
⋟sigh⋞

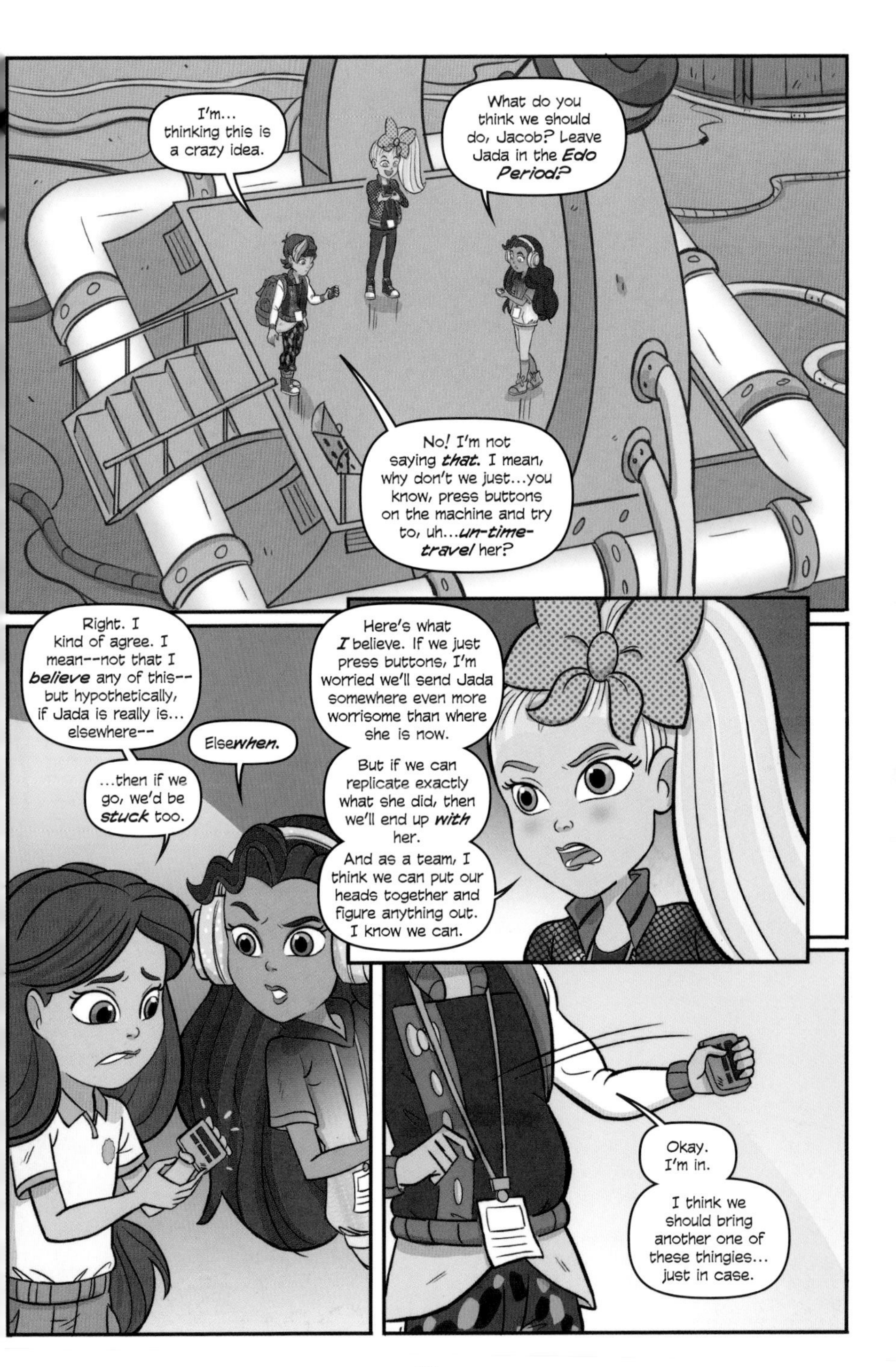
I'm... thinking this is a crazy idea.
What do you think we should do, Jacob? Leave Jada in the *Edo Period?*
No! I'm not saying *that.* I mean, why don't we just...you know, press buttons on the machine and try to, uh...*un-time-travel* her?
Right. I kind of agree. I mean--not that I *believe* any of this--but hypothetically, if Jada is really is... elsewhere--
Else*when.*
...then if we go, we'd be *stuck* too.
Here's what *I* believe. If we just press buttons, I'm worried we'll send Jada somewhere even more worrisome than where she is now.
But if we can replicate exactly what she did, then we'll end up *with* her.
And as a team, I think we can put our heads together and figure anything out. I know we can.
Okay. I'm in.
I think we should bring another one of these thingies... just in case.

Okay, so... she was over *here,* sort of tweaking this thing...and then she came over here, and she did a little *piano action* on these keys like this...
Oh, hey! Remember how she was holding her beeper when it all started?
She had it tucked like this.
I don't know if this is that important of a detail...
It's worth trying! The closer we get to doing *exactly* what she does, the better chance we have of getting to where she is now.
Come on... it has to work.

Dang. I don't know what else to press. I thought I did pretty much the same thing Jada did, but I guess--

Oh!
BEEP DEEP BADADA DEEP

Mine's lighting up!
Does this mean...
Come on, you guys. If this is a prank that you're in on, I give up. I don't want to joke around anymore...
BEEP DEEP BADADA DEEP
BEEP DEEP BADADA DEEP
BEEP DEEP BADADA DEEP

SHWAM
Ohhhh man! It feels like the gravitron!
Still think this is a prank, Caitlin?!
Here, grab on! We're doing this together.
Together.
Stop! I don't want to go! I don't want to!

Hey. Caitlin.
I got you, okay?
We're a team.
We're leaving as a team and we're coming back as a team.
BLTZ!

Oh...
My...
Actual...
Gosh.

We have to back up. We're...way, way, way too close to that thing!
It's the dinosaur from the museum! The one hanging from the ceiling, with the wings!
It's called a Pteranodon.
I can't believe my eyes.
Look a little closer.

Let's back up.
If it's protecting eggs,
I bet it'll be territorial.
We have to--
CRRKKK
Eeep!
Oh!

Can we stay and watch from here?
You are underestimating the danger of these times. This is *my* specialty so trust me...if *I'm* scared, you all should be freaking out.
Clearly something went *very, very wrong.* Jada is in the Edo period, and we are...we're in prehistoric times! This is *not good.*
Right, but *look.*
We're never going to get a chance to see something like this again, JoJo. *Please?*
I love you, girl, but it isn't safe here. We have to put our heads together and figure out these devices before we end up in a dangerous situation.
What's going to happen if we can't get back?
That is *not* a possibility, is it? JoJo, you know for *certain* that you pressed the exact same buttons that Jada did?
I know that I *tried.* Please, let's just calm down and *think* and--
COO!

AIIIIEEEEEEEEEE!
Oh, no.
Caitlin, wait! Don't run out into the open!
Come on, you stupid beeper! Work, work, work!
BEEP DEEP BADADA DEEP
coo!

Please, anywhere but here! Anywhere but where I'm dinosaur food!

Oh!
We're glowing! I see the pink light again! Everyone, grab hands, quick!

POK
Ow!
Caitlin, wait! Just grab my hand!
Aw, no!

BLTZ!
COO?

Is everyone okay? We're all together, all here?
Yeah... yeah, we're good.
But I think we better run.

JoJo, they saw us! Did we just break the timeline? Are we about to destroy the future and slowly vanish as our timeline collapses?
No! I...I mean, the truth is, I don't know how any of this works, but I promise you this.
You do not slowly vanish on my watch. You hear me, girl?
I hear you.
I'm so glad we all made it. When I realized we were about to...you know, time jump again, I was so worried we'd end up in separate places. Now we know we don't have to be touching.
I'm really sorry. I messed up. I panicked when I saw the dino and started pressing buttons...I promise I won't do that again.
But that could've gone a lot worse. We have to stick together. Remember, we're a team now.
I thought that was a--
...Oops.
I lost the other beeper. I fell and it went flying...and it's back with the dinosaurs.

It's okay, Jacob. You even having the idea to bring an extra one just in case was so nice. I'm a little worried about your leg, though.
Maybe we should get you to a doctor.
Excuse me, children.
Did I hear you say you need a doctor?

Apologies for eavesdropping.
I couldn't help myself but follow you after ...well, after I saw you appear from thin air.
If I hadn't seen you with my own eyes, I'd have never believed you were real...but here we are. Now, I must know your story.
I promise, I'm no journalist, if you're worried about this getting out.
Hi...to be honest, miss, I don't know for sure it's even safe for us to *interact* with people here.
Ah, yes. Your friend mentioned *vanishing*.
Though, we *do know* that Jada changed time by appearing in that Edo painting, right you guys? And she didn't destroy the world or anything.

My name is Dr. Susan Picotte. Maybe I could help your friend's leg if you spare some time to share your tale?

Susan Picotte? No way, as in Susan La Flesche Picotte?
How did you...

"You are an absolute inspiration, Dr. Picotte. You made history as one of the first Native Americans to earn a medical degree, and you did it in 1889.
"You were valedictorian of your class, too, at a time when women were thought to be less capable than men. You spoke three languages, became the only doctor on your reservation, and opened your own office nearby.
"You dreamed big and that means the world to me. Even though what I do is so different, I look toward women like you to inspire me to be the absolute best me that I can be."

That's so nice of you to say. I...find it hard to believe history has remembered me. Sometimes I don't even feel seen in the present.
I understand that for sure. But you help people.
Well, then let me help you and your friends here. We're just a couple of blocks away from my town office.
So this machinery that you use to make these "time jumps," as you put it...do any of you have any expertise whatsoever?
No. We didn't even know the machine existed until like an hour ago.
Well, I tend to think somewhat like your friend JoJo in this case. In an hour's time, you've done something completely new--and you've done it together.
I have the utmost faith that you'll locate your friend, wherever or whenever she is.
Do you mind if I take a quick look at your device?
Something you said on the way over here about the *sounds* it makes intrigued me.
Hmm.
DEEP-A-BEEP-DEEEEEEEEEEERP

The first time we time jumped, we held the beepers like *this.* Is that important?
DA DEEP!
Hmm.
Interesting. Each button seems to correspond to a different sound. The sounds change, too, when the button is held down.
Be careful, though, okay? I'd never forgive myself if I removed Susan Picotte from the timeline that needs her.
Do you hear it? The variety in the notes?
My brother Francis is an ***ethnomusicologist,*** and I play piano, so I suppose my ear is well trained.
He's a what now?
Ethnomusicologist. Basically, he studies music. He taught me quite a bit of what he knows, and I believe that what I heard from these devices are...musical notes. Do you know what musical notes correspond to?
Numbers.

Here. I've noticed how each button creates a sound that appears to be an octave higher than the previous.
This makes me believe that the buttons correspond to ***numbers.*** The lowest note is zero. The highest, nine.
I believe that, if you press these buttons, you will be able to select a year. That can help get you to the Edo Period. Within my notes, you can see which button I believe corresponds to each number.
Thank you so much.
When we first time jumped...and we didn't end up with Jada, I felt like my heart was going to break into a million pieces. I thought I led my friends astray.
I told them that we had to put our heads together and come up with a plan...and then we met you. And you did ***exactly that.***
My gosh, you had--I mean, have--everything stacked against you in life, in your career ...and you are an absolute ***giant*** in history. More than that, you ***truly*** help people. You helped ***me.***
And you are helping your friend.
If history knew what ***you*** were doing here today, you'd tower high as a giant yourself.
What you're doing takes immense bravery.
Thank you, Dr. Picotte. Thank you so much.

All right, I'm going to lead this time.
Based on the jump from the dinosaurs to now, we know that the devices will respond if just *one* of them is activated. All the others have to do is hold their device.
I'm going to set us to go to 1670...which is the last time we know that Jada was there. Dr. Picotte, can you just make sure that I'm getting the notes right?
I'm here for you, JoJo.
BEEP DEEP BADADA DEEP
It's happening!
THWAK!
coo!

YES!
IT WORKED!

CHAPTER THREE
JOJO & BASHŌ!

This is *ah-MAZING*, you guys. Not only did this work, but now we know something new about these devices.
That they're also kind of like musical instruments?
Well, *yes*, but also that there might somehow be *preprogrammed locations*.
All we've figured out how to do is *kind of* get to the correct year.
I wanted to end up in this year and then work on getting to Japan...but here we are, exactly where Jada was.
And now, we know that the beepers interact with each other, too.
If we can find Jada here, maybe we can all go back home together... *soon*.
I have a bad feeling about this. Back at the museum, I grabbed the extra beeper.
I kept thinking, "I feel like Jada's going to need this." And I lost it. I really messed up.
Jacob, no. She has her own. And if something happened to it, then we'll figure it out. It's *not* your fault.
None of this is anyone's fault.

Look, let's hide in that shop over there!
BLTZ!
coo?!
<Father, look! A dragon!>*
<Yeah, yeah, okay.>
*translated from Japanese

I think our best bet is to *limit* the amount of people we interact with.
Dr. Picotte was *amazing* and helpful, but we don't want someone reporting us to the authorities or something.
And gosh, if they find our phones... they're going to think we're *aliens*.
We *could* blend in a little better, I suppose. Hmm.
There's a booth that looks like it's selling clothes over there.
I don't know...I think we better just duck out of sight. How would we pay them?
True. But where do we go?
Look. The people working the booths are storing supplies between those tent flaps.
If we can get in there, we'd be able to run behind the booths and limit the people who see us.
Follow me!
This is the *first* and *only* time I've wished for *less* sequins on my outfit!

JoJo? Earth to JoJo? Time to get out of sight?

Sorry, I...I just got distracted.
Everything okay?
I think I recognize that man in there.
You're right. That's *Bashō*.
You were looking at his picture in the Edo exhibit when I met you.
I can't believe we're here right now.
I have an idea. Miley, come with me.
Jacob and Caitlin, can you two look around for Jada?
We'll meet back in front of this tent in ten minutes.
What's the plan?
Well... remember you were talking about your Japanese skills?
Oooooh boy.

Ahem.

Mr. Bashō? May I speak with you?

*Translated from Japanese
<Hello, sir. My name is Miley and this is my friend JoJo. Please excuse my Japanese. I am a student.>
<If you are okay with it, my friend would like to ask you some questions.>
<I can try to translate.>*

<I am happy to speak with you. It has been quite a slow day.>
Thank you so much. I'm sure once people realize how amazing your work is, they'll flock to you.

"Mr. Bashō, I read on your... I mean, I heard something about your work.
"I heard you're a very observant man, that you take in everything around you for your poetry.
"That spoke to me. I feel like people are so obsessed with trying to discover themselves sometimes that they forget that there's so much to discover out in the world."

So...I don't want to freak you out. But when I saw you, I knew in my heart that if my friend was here, you would've seen her.
You would've noticed her.
Please don't be scared of what I'm about to show you. It is a device from...from where I'm from. This will show you what my friend looks like.
<This...this item. What is it?>
Well, normally it's for communicating. But here, it doesn't really work. It also has pictures on it. Memories.
<Memories? Incredible. Where are you from, girls?>
I'll tell you everything, Mr. Bashō. But please...
Have you seen my friend?

Hm.
<I have seen this girl...and it makes an odd kind of sense that she is bonded in some way to you two.>
<You come to me in unusual garb and show me this wonder. An... an object beyond description.>
<Your friend caught my eye as she strolled down the street.>
<Her attire was strange...unlike anything I've ever seen.>
<It was no sooner that I stepped from my booth here to get a closer look...>
<...that this mysterious girl disappeared in a burst of pink light, like a flash of perfect sunset.>

COO!
<Hey! Keep your dogs leashed, man! He licks it, you buy it!>

Jada!
Jadaaaa!
Jada!
Hey, what's up? Need some energy? I'm still chock full of 'late.
That's short for chocolate, just so you know.
No, I just...I keep thinking...

I bet Jada knows exactly what she's doing. She's probably watching us right now, laughing, so she can punish me for doubting her.
Nah. You don't mean that.

What do you mean?
It's okay.
I feel guilty, too.

Come on. Let's get back to the others.

What I do...it's very different. But I write lyrics, too. I...
It's so odd. Seeing your work makes me feel so inspired, but it also makes me feel so far from home.
It's only been a day, but I feel like I haven't been home in years.

I thought we would've found her by now.

<You said earlier that I am... an observer. It's true. Part of that observing, though, is *waiting*. To sit, to ponder, to observe, and to *think*...>

<It is not the same as inaction. Merely being together, you and your friends here, is an act of love for this lost girl.>
You're right. That's true.
Thank you.

Wait a second...*being together*.
I think I have an idea.

So we know now that the beepers don't have to all enter in a timeline in order for the full set to travel there.
But you know what? I think they have to be *held*.

I think there's some kind of communication between the beepers that is only active when someone is holding them. Think about it.

"All of the beepers **except** Jada's were still there after her jump.

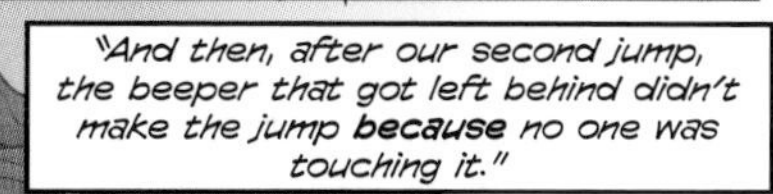
"And then, after our second jump, the beeper that got left behind didn't make the jump **because** no one was touching it."

Mr. Bashō, the idea you just gave me...I think it's going to save my friend.
<I don't understand...but after what I have seen, I believe.>
What if, wherever Jada is, the reason that she isn't time jumping with us is because she wasn't touching her beeper at the moments we made the jumps?
Wait, so what do we do?
But if we can't communicate with her, how do we get her to touch the beeper at the right moment.
We don't.
"We hold our beepers. Hard. Never letting go. Not until Jada makes a new jump...because we already know that she figured out how to leave here. Bashō saw it.
"If these devices are really connected, and I think they are...all we have to do is wait."

Oh!
Miley, Jacob, Caitlin! It's happening! Are you holding your beepers?
This is it! If I'm right... this is truly it.
Yes!

Mr. Bashō...thank you so much. For your words, for your patience, for your inspiration.
<And thank you for yours.>
<I will write of you...and your friend.>

Wait...
what?
I...I don't think she's here, JoJo.
She has to be. It--it doesn't make sense if she's not.
JADA!
JADA?!
Jada...please... please be here... Why didn't it work? How...how did we even make the jump if she didn't do it?
JoJo... if she's not...
She *will* be.
If she's not...just trust me on this.
There is *no one* I know who would do a better job of figuring out what to do next than you.
You *will* find her.
Look how far you already got us. I believe in you.

He's right, JoJo.
But you don't have to worry anymore. I'm here.

JADA!
I am so beyond happy to see you.
You are never allowed to time travel without us again! Are you okay?
Are you okay?
Well...I **was.**
"I've been trying to get my time jumps closer and closer to our time, but I haven't exactly figured out the programming yet...so I think I just cut back from the '50s to now...
"...which I'm **pretty** sure is the 1940s.
ALL-AMERICAN GIRLS PROFESSIONAL BASEBALL LEAGUE
"Annnnd this last jump for some reason dropped me on top of a bench in the dugout. I fell as soon as I landed and broke my remote."
Jada, I...I brought an extra--I mean, I **tried,** but...I left it behind. I feel so, so bad. I knew something was going to happen to you. I had a feeling.
I'm so impressed that you managed to even get here. I mean, I'm...I just **can't believe** you're here. I have so many questions.
This is **my exhibit** and I started out just... completely lost.

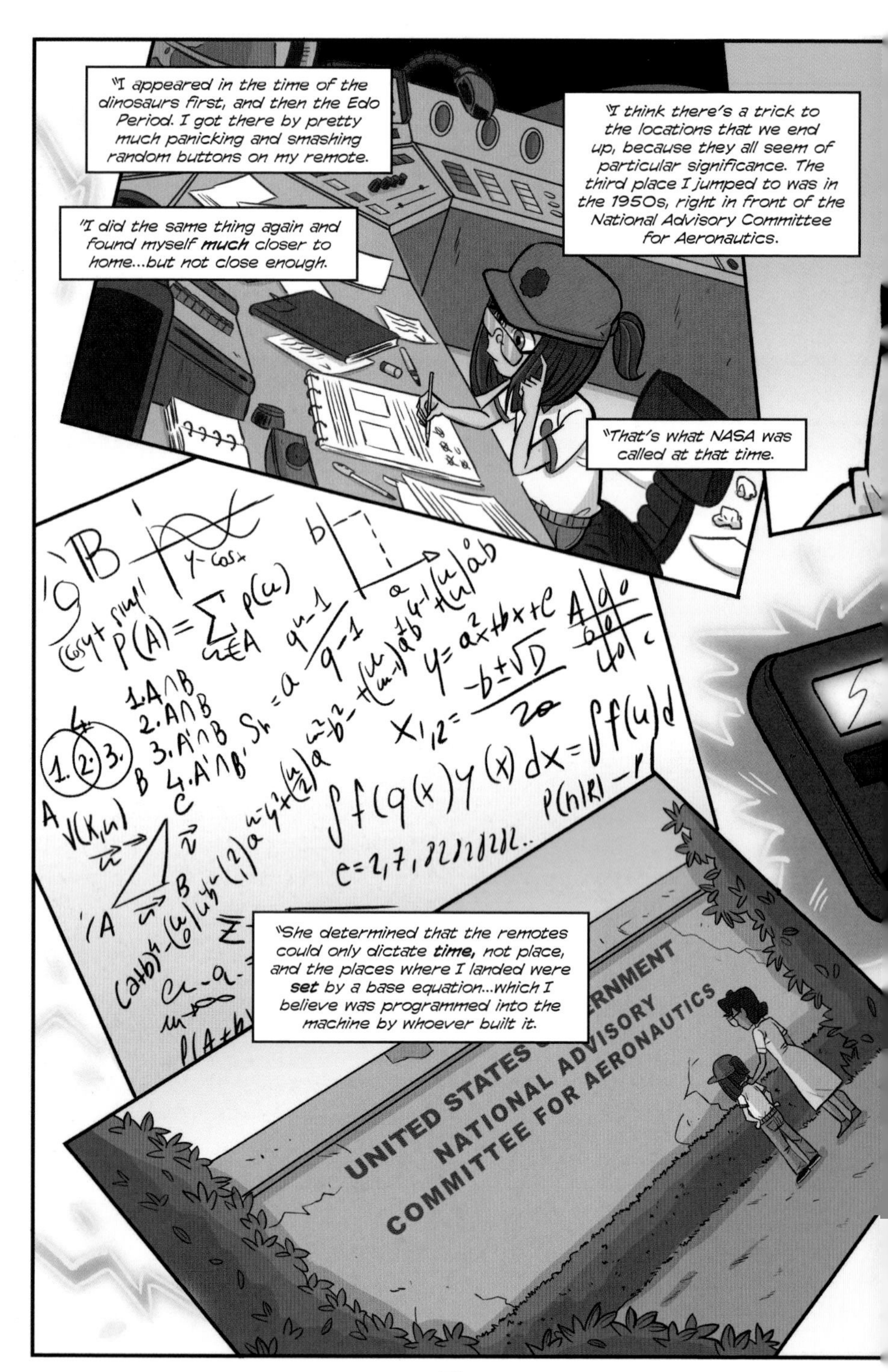
"I appeared in the time of the dinosaurs first, and then the Edo Period. I got there by pretty much panicking and smashing random buttons on my remote.
"I did the same thing again and found myself **much** closer to home...but not close enough.
"I think there's a trick to the locations that we end up, because they all seem of particular significance. The third place I jumped to was in the 1950s, right in front of the National Advisory Committee for Aeronautics.
"That's what NASA was called at that time.
"She determined that the remotes could only dictate **time,** not place, and the places where I landed were **set** by a base equation...which I believe was programmed into the machine by whoever built it.
UNITED STATES GOVERNMENT
NATIONAL ADVISORY
COMMITTEE FOR AERONAUTICS

"I met a brilliant mathematician named **Katherine Johnson**--the first African-American woman to work as a NASA scientist!
"Knowing that her equations would be used to make advances in spacecrafts, I was certain she could help me.
"Katherine Johnson gave me her equations and I made my next jump, left speechless by her genius."

"In my attempt to move forward through time, I went backward instead...and when I found myself in 1830s London, I wondered if I dared approach the one woman of that time I believed could help me.
"Ada Lovelace.
"Lovelace is seen by many as the first computer programmer.
"She thought I was crazy...but all I had to do was show her Katherine Johnson's notes.
"Genius recognizes genius.

"From there, she helped me figure out a pattern in the buttons that helped me get a rough understanding of moving forward in time rather than back. Ever since then, I've always gotten within ten years of my target jump."

That's brilliant, Jada. We also made friends and I think, with what *we* learned and what you learned...we can finally get back home.

CHAPTER FOUR
HOME RUN

Hey, youse girls!
Whaddaya doin'?! Get the heck off the field!
Is--is something about to happen here?
You guys...I recognize that man. Jada, do you remember the sports exhibit that was running when you first started working at the museum?
I do! Oh, my gosh, is that--
EDDIE STUMPF!
The coach of the Rockford Peaches, one of the first teams in the All-American Girls Professional Baseball League.
We *can* program our remotes to get home any time we want, right?
Theoretically, if we do it right. Why?

"'Cause I wanna stay for the game!"
PEACHES! PEACHES!

STRIKE TWO!
GPBL

STRIKE THREE!
Aw, this is kind of a bummer. The Peaches are losing...

Hmm. Maybe they need some inspiration.

VELMA ABBOTT, UP AT BAT!
Hey! Velma! Er, Ms. Abbott!
Not the best time for distraction, blondie.
For sure! I just--I just wanted to say, because of what women like you are doing right now, girls like me are going to be able to live their lives knowing there is absolutely no limit to their awesomeness.
That's all!
...All right, kid. Thanks.

CRACK
AND AGAINST ALL ODDS, VELMA ABBOTT OF THE ROCKFORD PEACHES HITS A GRAND SLAM!

IT LOOKS LIKE THE PEACHES HAVE THIS GAME IN THE BAG, LADIES AND GENTLEMEN!
Woooh-hoo!

So you're saying that the buttons of the remote correlate to *musical notes?* That's...I never would've thought of that.
Yeah! We've been able to get super specific with our jumps, thanks to Dr. Picotte.
I'm *pretty* sure we can just go right to our time.
Fingers crossed that the museum is one of those preprogrammed locations.
Imagine we end up in like, modern-day *Alaska?* Brrr.
So here's the issue we have to figure out.
We need to get a few of us to the museum in our time, and then someone needs to come back to *this* time with another remote for Jada to--
She can have mine!

Jada can have my beeper. Er, remote.
I'm the reason we're here at all. And I'm *sorry.*
I trust that you'll come back for me, but please...Jada, you deserve to go home first.
You were alone, and...I can't imagine how scary it was for you.

Caitlin, I--
Seeing how everyone keeps working together, it's just...It's what I should've done with you at the museum.

"I was there before you, and when you came in...I guess I felt threatened by you.
"Your exhibit is so unique and fun and just...it seemed like people were excited about your work. Like, mine was just...it was just what people expected.
"I got too defensive...because I *love* what I do. But I know you do, too, and...I'm just sorry."
Please. I'll be part of the team now.
You go and I'll be here when you're ready to get me.

You don't have to, Caitlin. I'm *fine.* I could just hang back while--
No.
Please.
You *are* part of the team. And we *will* be back for you.
Everything we learned, we learned together. Through mistakes, through inspiration...we did it, all of us, all the people we met, together.
We'll bring back an extra remote, and then we'll go home *together*.
A A
GPBL

Thank you, Caitlin. We'll be right back.
AIEEEEEE! IT FOLLOWED US! IT'S HUNTING US!
coo?

Wait a second...
Hey...You're a *triceratops*, aren't you, little guy?
I didn't get a good look either during our first jump. Everything was so weird and tense that I wanted to run.

But, cute as he is...*how* is he here?

You guys...I think I figured out the mystery of the missing remote. I'm *pretty* sure it's in our friend's belly here.
I have an idea. Just a very, very friendly surprise that could mayyyybe surprise it out of him?
Sort of like a hiccup cure...but y'know, *JoJo style*.
You all be super quiet around him. It needs to be ***peeeeaceful*** for this to work.
Shhhhh little baby, *shhhhh*.
Ahem.

HIGH NOTEEEEEE!

coo?
I have an idea.
"I used to babysit my cousin all the time. I am very experienced with burping a baby."
And this is a baby!

PAT
PAT
BURP!
Oh, foul...
It's just as well. As long as it's not hurting him, he needs to get back to his own time before any more people see him than already have.
We don't know if changing time creates, like... splinter timelines, right?
Well, if it did, we've created a **ton** of new realities. So...I guess, ***you're welcome,*** alternate reality people who now exist because of us?
But no, I have no idea about any of that. But I do agree--best to limit the "I saw a dinosaur" folks to all present. Let's make the jump.
I'll see you all soon.

All right. Adorable dino: returned. Now, homeward bound.
Hey, actually...
BLTZ!
Remember how you said before the game that we could program our jumps for *any* time?
Doesn't that mean we actually *do* end up having time to catch this absolute *miracle of life?*
You know what, Miley?
Yes, it does.
There, look! It's hatching!

CRR
CRR
RRRK
CRRKKK

coo
Aw, I'm going to miss him. I think he thought I was his mom.
Maybe he--
BERRRRP!
Snff snff
Oh, boy. Well...it looks like we have an extra remote now.
DEEP-A-BEEP-DEEEEEEEEEEEERP
Ew, what the heck is that *smell?!*

Okay. Clean as it's gonna be. Let's just make this quick.
You know what? We're going to remember this...all of the stress...and yes, even this...for the rest of our lives. I can't believe we got to do this.
And I'm so glad we're all okay.
BLTZ!

Hey, friend.

BLTZ!
Ohmigosh, we did it!
Woooooh!
What's that smell?
We're home.

Caitlin, I wanted to say...I'm sorry about this, too. All of you, I'm sorry. You came back and you saved me, but I shouldn't have been messing around with this to begin with.
I'm going to request they shut down the exhibit. Maybe I can move to where you are, Caitlin, and help you out.
Jada, you can do what you feel is best and I'll support you...but I meant what I said.
"What we experienced was... well, as a great man told me today, it was beyond description.
"Beyond even his words, which is saying a lot.
"Here's the thing about what we went through. It was scary, yes. There were a few times where I didn't know what to do.
"But the whole time, even when we were apart...we had each other, and we were able to find inspiration everywhere, and like Miley said, everywhen."
All of this...what happened to us, our friendship... it's not something that is your fault. It's something I celebrate.

"These memories and all this history...it's part of us now.

"And we're part of it."
END.

MEET THE REAL-LIFE HISTORICAL FIGURES OF *THE TERRIFIC TIME TWIST*

ADA LOVELACE

The first computer programmer! Way back in 1842, Ada Lovelace created a program for a prototype of a digital computer. Many people thought computers were only good for number crunching, but she foresaw people using them to connect and work together in many different ways. To learn more, be sure to read another book from Abrams Books for Young Readers, *Ada's Ideas!*

MATSUO BASHŌ

Matsuo Bashō was considered both the most famous poet in Japan during the Edo period (between 1603 and 1867) and the absolute master of the haiku. He perfected his writing while adventuring, wandering around Japan and through the wilderness while using what he saw and felt as inspiration for his poems.

KATHERINE JOHNSON

Katherine Johnson was a Black mathematician famous for both loving math and helping send people into space! As a girl, she counted everything, even the dishes in her sink, and went to college at just fifteen years old! She later joined NASA and solved extremely tough math problems that helped the first expedition to the moon to get there and come back safely.

Susan La Flesche Picotte

Dr. Susan La Flesche Picotte was one of the first Native Americans to earn a medical degree, and a tireless reformer! She fought hard against then-incurable diseases such as tuberculosis and worked to protect land rights for her Omaha tribe. She helped many people live long and healthy lives—she was the sole doctor for her reservation of twelve hundred people and ran a clinic in town, too.

All-American Girls Professional Baseball League

This amazing team was one of the first of many women's pro sports teams. There were over six hundred women in the AAGPBL—and they sure knew how to draw a crowd, with over 900,000 people watching their games! The Rockford Peaches team was especially successful, setting a league-record for winning four championships.

Triceratops

"Triceratops"—which literally means "three-horned face"—is a dinosaur known for its three-horned skull, rhino-like body, and bony, frilly neck. It first appeared in what we now call North America over sixty-eight million years ago! And even though it's much bigger than other dinos, the triceratops prefers to eat plants.

Want more JoJo?

Enjoy a sample chapter from

Razzle-Dazzle Babysitters!

7

JoJo & Bow Bow

RAZZLE-DAZZLE BABYSITTERS

BY JOJO SIWA

nickelodeon

CHAPTER 1

"I'm still not sure why you set up this emergency get-together at Maria's Pizza," JoJo said, smiling at her best friend, Miley, as she helped herself to a slice of pepperoni pizza, "but I definitely approve of the location!"

JoJo sighed happily as she inhaled the delicious aroma of fresh-from-the-oven pizza. She could tell by the steam coming off her slice that it was still too hot to taste. She took another look at Miley. "I also approve of that new hairstyle you've got going on," JoJo added. Miley had the top section of her long, wavy dark hair pulled into a messy bun with a velvet scrunchie, leaving the bottom part cascading around her shoulders.

"Aww, thanks! You always notice when something is even a teeny bit different," Miley commented.

"As your BFF, it's my job to notice these things," JoJo joked. "Seriously, though, Miley, what's up? Everything okay?"

Miley nodded as she fanned a hand over her own slice, trying to cool it off. "Everything is fine! I just felt like I needed a little break. With homework, choreography stuff, visiting Dusty, and ice-skating lessons, it seemed like I hadn't seen you in forever! Then I remembered that we had yet to try this place, which is supposed to be the best new spot in town, and thought a pizza date sounded like the perfect idea!"

"Pizza dates are always a perfect idea!" JoJo agreed. "And good for you for knowing when to say you need a break." JoJo paused and lowered her voice. "Although . . . not that I'm complaining . . . but we did just see each other over the weekend!"

"Really?" Miley burst into giggles. "Well it *felt* like forever!"

"Did you girls try the pizza yet?" Mrs. McKenna asked from the neighboring table. "It lives up to the hype!" Miley's mom often let the girls sit together at their own table in restaurants while she sat nearby and caught up on work emails. They would not have minded one bit if she sat with them, of course, but both JoJo and Miley appreciated the private time together.

"I've waited long enough. I'm going in!" JoJo announced. She carefully folded her slice, raised it to her mouth, and took a big bite. A slow smile spread over her face. "Oh em gee, this might be the best pizza *ever*. It's got the perfect cheese-to-sauce ratio, and the crust is . . ." JoJo opened her eyes and realized Miley wasn't even paying attention! She was twisted around in her seat, looking toward the front of the restaurant.

"Don't look now, but I'm pretty sure Goldie Chic just walked in!" Miley whispered.

"Really?" JoJo tried to look casual as she leaned out of the booth to scope things out.

"I think you're right," she said a moment later. The famous designer had such a unique look that JoJo doubted it could be anyone other than her. From her signature long brown hair to her gold bangles to her glittery cat-eye glasses, the tall woman at the front of the restaurant looked *exactly* like Goldie Chic.

"She has a little girl with her. Is that her daughter?" JoJo knew a lot about Goldie because her friend Kyra was a huge fan of hers, but she couldn't remember if the designer had a daughter.

"I think so. I can't *believe* Kyra's not here with us," Miley cried, as if reading JoJo's mind. "Maybe we can ask her for an autograph for Kyra after she sits down. What do you think?"

JoJo thought about it. As someone who was often asked for her autograph, she knew how great it felt to meet and connect with a fan. On the other hand, maybe Goldie just wanted to have a quiet dinner with her daughter.

But JoJo didn't have to decide because a moment later Goldie Chic and her daughter stopped by *their* table!

"I'm so sorry to interrupt your meal,"

Goldie said smoothly, a friendly smile lighting up her face. "But my niece back in New York is a huge fan of yours, JoJo! Can I get your autograph for her?"

"Of course!" JoJo exclaimed. She scooted over in her seat in the booth. "Would you like to sit down for a minute?"

Goldie looked over at Mrs. McKenna, who nodded and smiled, and then gracefully slid into the booth.

"This is my best friend Miley"—JoJo gestured to Miley as she introduced her—"and that's her mom, Mrs. McKenna, in the next booth."

"It's so nice to meet all of you!" Goldie exclaimed. "And this"—she bounced the little girl on her lap—"is Lacey."

"Hi!" Lacey exclaimed, waving to everyone.

"Hi, there," JoJo said, waving back. "It's nice to meet you!"

Lacey grinned and then buried her head in her mother's ruffled blouse.

"Are you feeling a little shy?" JoJo asked. Lacey peeked her head out, giggled, and then buried her head again.

"So we saw you come in and were going to ask for *your* autograph for our friend Kyra," Miley explained as JoJo fished a pad of paper out of her pink-striped backpack. "We were just discussing whether it would be okay to say hi when you walked over!"

"I always love meeting fans," Goldie replied graciously. "But I appreciate that you were so thoughtful about it. Unlike me, just barging over here and interrupting your meal! But my niece would probably disown me if she ever found out I was in the same place as JoJo Siwa and didn't get an autograph!"

JoJo grinned. "What's your niece's name?"

“Vienna,” Goldie replied. “Can I have a sheet of paper to autograph for your friend? Her name’s Kyra?”

“Yep, Kyra.” Miley nodded. “She’s a designer too, and a huge fan of yours! She was telling me how you started designing when you were about our age . . .”

JoJo snuck a smile at Miley as she wrote a message to Vienna. Miley was a pretty big fan of Goldie’s too, but she was using her time with Goldie to talk up Kyra. Reason number 4, 237 why Miley was such an amazing friend!

JoJo finished with the autograph for Vienna and slid it, an extra piece of paper, and the pen over to Goldie.

“We draw now?” Lacey asked, her eyes lighting up as she watched the exchange.

“Not now, sweetheart,” Goldie said. But Lacey had already wrapped her little fingers around the pen.

"I have plenty of paper . . . ," JoJo said quietly so Lacey couldn't hear her. "And a bunch of colored pencils in my bag. Just sayin' . . ."

"Oh, okay!" Goldie laughed as Lacey clutched the pen in her fist like it was a treasure she would never let go of.

"Can I trade you that one pen for all these colored pencils?" JoJo asked Lacey.

Lacey's eyes widened when she saw the handful of brightly colored pencils JoJo was offering. She promptly dropped the pen. JoJo retrieved it and then spread out the pencils on the table in front of Lacey so she could begin drawing.

"And here is the autograph for Kyra," Goldie said a few moments later after writing a message to Kyra and signing her name with flourish.

"I love your bag," JoJo exclaimed to Goldie as she tucked the autograph in the front pocket of her own backpack. "Miley, it kind of reminds me of that scarf Kyra designed . . ."

"Absolutely!" Miley agreed.

"So Kyra designs scarves?" Goldie asked. "Is she only into accessories, or clothes too?"

"She does it all," Miley said. As Miley explained some of Kyra's work, JoJo pulled her phone out of her bag. She scrolled through the photos to look for the shots of her and her friends wearing the outfits Kyra had designed for Miley's birthday party.

"Here are some pics of ice-skating costumes she designed," JoJo said, trying to hand her phone to Goldie.

"Play games!" Lacey cried, reaching for JoJo's phone.

"Oh no, sweetie, that's JoJo's phone," Goldie said, gently prying Lacey's fingers away from the phone. "She just wants to show Mommy something."

Lacey's face scrunched up.

"Will you do something for me?" JoJo asked, sliding the phone over to Miley so it would be out of Lacey's line of sight.

Lacey frowned, and her lip trembled a bit. JoJo knew that toddlers had a hard time with being told "no," and she had just a few moments to distract her before she possibly melted down.

"Will you draw me a picture?" JoJo continued. "Just for me, and I can keep it forever?"

"Of what?" Lacey asked.

"Hmmm . . . how about a pizza? With sprinkles and ice cream on top?"

Lacey clapped her hands and started drawing.

"You're so good with her," Goldie exclaimed as she accepted the phone from Miley under the table. "It's a shame you're not a little older—I'd hit you up for babysitting!"

"Aw, thanks," JoJo replied. "I love little kids."

Goldie nodded as she scrolled through the photos. "Wow, she's really talented," she said a minute later. "I'm loving that glitter edging she did. That's a really hard detail to do . . ." She looked more closely at one of the photos. "But that bomber jacket she made for your guy friend? That's the bomb dot com!"

"Right?" JoJo and Miley exclaimed at the same time.

Goldie smiled and handed the phone back to JoJo. "Your friend has a lot of talent. Please tell her I said so!"

"I wish she was here so you could tell her in person," Miley replied.

"We will make sure to bring Kyra with us on all future pizza outings, just in case we ever run in to you again," JoJo joked.

"Sounds like a plan." Goldie laughed. "Though going out tonight was a rare treat for me. I'm in the middle of launching my new collection and have been working non-stop. And I need to find a babysitter for Lacey. We just moved here from New York, and I don't have one yet." Hearing her name, Lacey looked up from the picture she was drawing to smile at everyone and then went back to drawing. "Do you girls happen to have any friends who are a little older and into babysitting by any chance?"

"It's too bad you need someone older," JoJo responded. "Kyra is practically a pro with kids!"

"I have a suggestion," Mrs. McKenna said, leaning over from the neighboring booth. "When Miley was little, the girl who lived next door used to do some supervised babysitting for me. She'd come over and play with Miley while I was home so there was still an adult present, but it was enough of a relief for me that I could get stuff done. And Miley loved it because she got to hang out with an older girl."

"That could work . . . ," Goldie said, nodding her head. " And is Kyra as good with kids as you are, JoJo?"

JoJo grinned. "She *loves* kids! She's done some supervised babysitting for our friend Jacob's little brother. I have to check with her, but I'm sure she'll be on board!"

"Great, let's make it happen!" Goldie said.

Lacey looked up from her drawing and grinned. "Let's make it happen!" she repeated.

"I think we're going to have our hands full with this little cutie!" JoJo laughed.

FIND OUT WHAT HAPPENS NEXT IN *RAZZLE-DAZZLE BABYSITTERS!*

More books available . . .

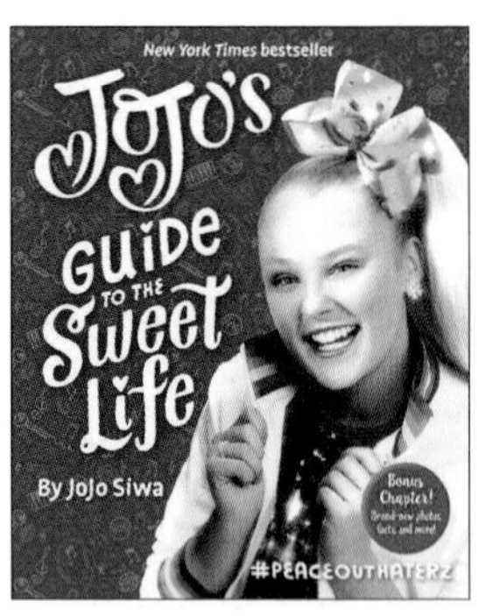

. . . BY JOJO SIWA!

JoJo & Bow Bow
THE POSH PUPPY PAGEANT
BY JOJO SIWA
nickelodeon

JoJo & Bow Bow
SLUMBER PARTY SPARKLES
BY JOJO SIWA

JoJo & Bow Bow
QUEEN B's AND HONEYBEES
BY JOJO SIWA

JoJo & Bow Bow
THE GREAT BEACH CAKE BAKE
BY JOJO SIWA
nickelodeon

JoJo & Bow Bow
RAZZLE-DAZZLE BABYSITTERS
BY JOJO SIWA
nickelodeon

JoJo & Bow Bow
SPRING BREAK DOUBLE TAKE
BY JOJO SIWA
nickelodeon

JoJo & Bow Bow
JINGLE BOWS AND MISTLETOE
SUPER SPECIAL
BY JOJO SIWA
nickelodeon

JoJo & Bow Bow
THE GHOSTESS WITH THE MOSTEST
SUPER SPECIAL
BY JOJO SIWA
nickelodeon